# Praise Song for the Day

beth Alexander

## A Poem for Barack Obama's Presidential Inauguration

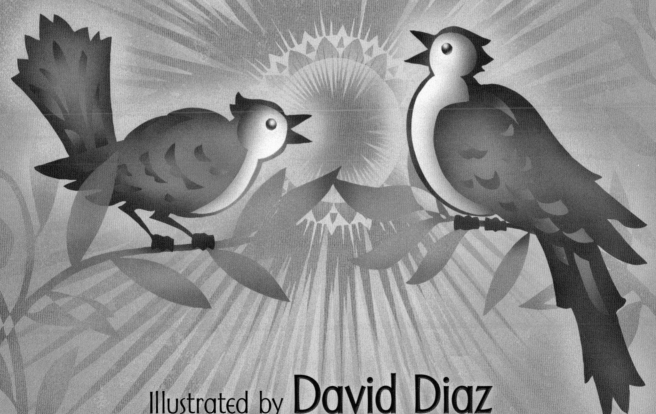

Illustrated by David Diaz

 KATHERINE TEGEN BOOKS
*An Imprint of HarperCollins Publishers*

The poem *Praise Song for the Day* was first published by Graywolf Press.

Katherine Tegen Books is an imprint of HarperCollins Publishers.

Praise Song for the Day: A Poem for Barack Obama's Presidential Inauguration
Text copyright © 2009 by Elizabeth Alexander
Illustrations copyright © 2012 by David Diaz

Library of Congress Cataloging-in-Publication Data is available.
ISBN 978-0-06-192663-1

Typography by Martha Rago
12 13 14 15 16  SCP  10 9 8 7 6 5 4 3 2 1
❖
First Edition

For Elise
—D.D.

Each day we go about our business,
walking past each other, catching each other's
eyes or not, about to speak or speaking.

All about us is noise. All about us is noise and bramble, thorn and din, each one of our ancestors on our tongues.

Someone is stitching up a hem, darning a hole in a uniform, patching a tire, repairing the things in need of repair.

Someone is trying to make music somewhere,
with a pair of wooden spoons on an oil drum,
with cello, boom box, harmonica, voice.

A woman and her son wait for the bus.
A farmer considers the changing sky.
A teacher says, *Take out your pencils. Begin.*

We encounter each other in words, words
spiny or smooth, whispered or declaimed,
words to consider, reconsider.

We cross dirt roads and highways that mark
the will of someone and then others, who said
I need to see what's on the other side.

I know there's something better down the road.
We need to find a place where we are safe.
We walk into that which we cannot yet see.

Say it plain: that many have died for this day.
Sing the names of the dead who brought us here,
who laid the train tracks, raised the bridges,

picked the cotton and the lettuce, built
brick by brick the glittering edifices
they would then keep clean and work inside of.

Praise song for struggle, praise song for the day.
Praise song for every hand-lettered sign,
the figuring it out at kitchen tables.

Some live by *love thy neighbor as thyself*,
others by *first do no harm* or *take no more
than you need*. What if the mightiest word is love?

Love beyond marital, filial, national,
love that casts a widening pool of light,
love with no need to preempt grievance.

In today's sharp sparkle, this winter air,
any thing can be made, any sentence begun.
On the brink, on the brim, on the cusp,

praise song for walking forward in that light.